PEEK-A-BOO
BUNNY

For the gorgeous Ava-Lucia:
hop little bunny, hop hop hop! xxx

Also by Holly Surplice:

ABOUT A BEAR

Peek-a-Boo Bunny
Copyright © 2013 by Holly Surplice
All rights reserved. Manufactured in China.
No part of this book may be used or reproduced in any manner whatsoever without written permission except
in the case of brief quotations embodied in critical articles and reviews. For information address HarperCollins
Children's Books, a division of HarperCollins Publishers, 10 East 53rd Street, New York, NY 10022.
www.harpercollinschildrens.com

ISBN 978-0-06-224265-5 (trade bdg.)

The artist used mixed media and collage to create the illustrations for this book.
13 14 15 16 17 SCP 10 9 8 7 6 5 4 3 2 1
❖
First U.S. edition, 2014
Originally published in the U.K. by HarperCollins Children's Books, 2013

PEEK-A-BOO
BUNNY

Holly Surplice

HARPER

An Imprint of HarperCollinsPublishers

Bunny's with his
friends today,

and there's one game they
LOVE to play!

Bunny,
    Bunny,
        don't you peek. . . .

Bunny, Bunny, hide and seek!

Bunny
jumping on
the spot.

Bunny coming, ready or not!

Bunny, Bunny
running fast,
rushes by
and speeds
right past.

Bunny hopping here
and there. . . .

Bunny, Bunny
misses Hare.

Bunny, Bunny
sniffs around,

but does not like
the smell he's found!

Bunny, trying
not to fall,

misses friends
both big
and small.

Bunny busy stretching high,
doesn't see what Mole can spy.

Bunny searching on the ground—

if only he would
turn around!

Bunny, Bunny
looking down—

his smile
is turning
to a frown.

Bunny,
Bunny, what
to do?

Bunny, Bunny . . .